For Lani-Grace and Solomon
with biggest bestest love.
PS Don't forget your mummies
were once Double Trouble! A

✳

To Elizabeth and Andrew Viney,
with love. L.T.

First American Edition 2015
Kane Miller, A Division of EDC Publishing

Text © 2015 Atinuke
Illustrations © 2015 Lauren Tobia

Published by arrangement with Walker Books Ltd
87 Vauxhall Walk, London SE11 5HJ

For information contact:
Kane Miller, A Division of EDC Publishing
PO Box 470663
Tulsa, OK 74147-0663
www.kanemiller.com
www.edcpub.com
www.usbornebooksandmore.com

Library of Congress Control Number: 2014947160

Printed in China
1 2 3 4 5 6 7 8 9 10

ISBN: 978-1-61067-367-9

DOUBLE TROUBLE
FOR ANNA HIBISCUS!

ATINUKE ✳ LAUREN TOBIA

Anna Hibiscus
lives in Africa.
Amazing Africa.

"Anna Hibiscus,"
Papa whispers.
"Come and see..."

"Babies!" says Anna. "Two babies!"

"Your brothers, Anna Hibiscus."
Mama smiles.

"It is brothers," Anna Hibiscus tells her cousins.

"That big bump was brothers."

"Boys!" shouts Benz.

"Two boys!" whispers Angel.

"That means trouble!" says Clarity.

"Big Trouble!" says Chocolate.

"Uh-oh," thinks Anna Hibiscus.

Anna Hibiscus runs back to Mama
for her morning cuddle.

"Mama is sleeping now," whispers Papa.
"Your brothers have worn her out!"

"Uh-oh," thinks Anna Hibiscus again.
"Maybe they are trouble."

Anna Hibiscus goes down to the kitchen
for breakfast. Anna Hibiscus always
has ogi for breakfast. Uncle Bizi Sunday always
makes it for her.
But Uncle Bizi Sunday is busy.
Busy making food for Anna's mother.

"She is now eating for three!"
Uncle Bizi Sunday says.

"They *are* trouble,"
thinks Anna Hibiscus.

Anna Hibiscus takes a big ripe banana.
She goes to Grandmother's mat.
Anna Hibiscus always eats breakfast
with Grandmother.

But Grandmother is busy sleeping.

"Grandmother was up all night,"
whispers Joy.

"Helping your brothers to be born,"
whispers Common Sense.

"More trouble!"
thinks Anna Hibiscus.

Anna Hibiscus goes outside to eat her banana.
The aunties are outside. They always wash clothes
in the morning, and they always let Anna Hibiscus help.

But the aunties are not washing clothes!
They are busy rocking the babies.

"Shh..." they whisper.

"It's not easy getting babies to sleep,"
whispers Auntie Grace.

"Trouble again!" shouts Anna Hibiscus.
She shouts so loudly
the babies start to cry.

Anna Hibiscus runs to hide
before the aunties can be cross with her.

Anna Hibiscus is lonely hiding.
She thinks of the uncles.
The uncles always have time to play.

But the uncles are busy too!

"Those brothers of yours have given
us a lot to do!" says Uncle Habibi.

"Double the work," says Uncle Tunde.

"Double trouble!"
shouts Anna Hibiscus.

Anna Hibiscus starts to cry.

"Wha' happen?" Papa asks.

"Everybody is busy with Double Trouble!"
cries Anna Hibiscus.
"Nobody has time for me."

"Double trouble?" Papa asks.

"Those babies!"
says Anna Hibiscus.
"Those brothers!"

Papa laughs!
"You will have to share us with your
brothers, Anna," he says.

"But it's not fair!"
cries Anna Hibiscus.

"Anna Hibiscus!"
It is Uncle Bizi Sunday calling.
"Your ogi is ready now!"

"Anna!" Grandmother is calling too.
"I am waiting to eat with you!"

"We are going to need your help
with the washing, Anna Hibiscus,"
the aunties say.

"Then we will take you
to the water park."
The uncles smile. "All of you!"

"Hooray!"
shout all the cousins.
"Hurry, Anna!"

"You see." Papa smiles.
"Everybody has time
for Anna Hibiscus!"

Anna Hibiscus smiles too.

Then she looks at her brothers.
They are still crying.

Anna Hibiscus kisses one brother.
"Don't cry, little Trouble," she says.

Anna Hibiscus kisses the other brother.
"Don't cry, little Double," she says.

"We have Mama and Papa,
  and Grandmother and Grandfather,
  and so many aunties and uncles
  and cousins to share!
  You don't need to cry."

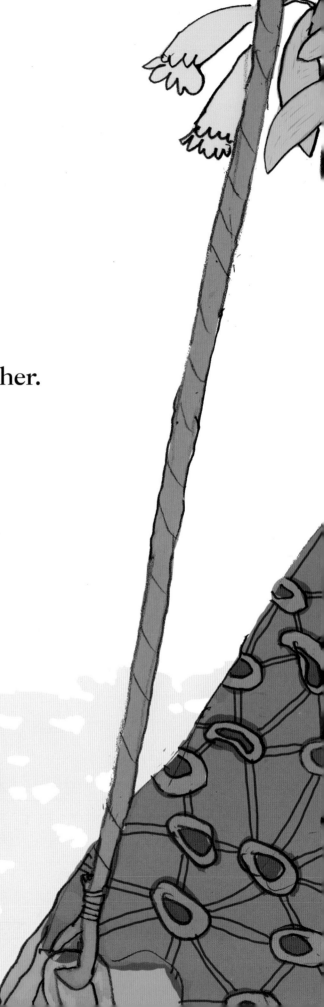

Anna Hibiscus is
so happy now!

She is going to eat ogi
with Grandmother,
splash with her aunties,
and play with her uncles
and cousins.

But first Anna Hibiscus
runs to her mother.

"Are you busy?"
  Anna Hibiscus asks.

"Busy cuddling you, Anna Hibiscus,"
  her mother says.

"Welcome to our family,
Double Trouble!"
says Anna Hibiscus.

Anna Hibiscus lives in Africa.
Amazing Africa.
Anna Hibiscus is amazing too.